Usborne Farmyard Tales Sticker Stories

The New Pony

Heather Amery

Illustrated by Stephen Cartwright

Language consultant: Betty Root
Series editor: Jenny Tyler

How to use this book

This book tells a story about the Boot family. They live on Apple Tree Farm.
Some words in the story have been replaced by pictures.
Find the stickers that match these pictures and stick them on top.
Each sticker has the word with it to help you read the story.

Some of the big pictures have pieces missing.
Find the stickers with the missing pieces to finish the pictures.

A yellow duck is hidden in every picture. When you have found
the duck you can put a   sticker on the page.

Sam

I found the duck!

This is Apple Tree Farm.

Mrs. Boot, the farmer, has two

children

called Poppy and Sam. She also has a

dog

called Rusty.

2

Poppy and Sam go for a walk.

Mr. Boot goes with them. They see a pony

looking over a 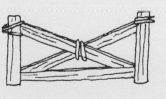 . "She belongs

to Mr. Stone," says

The pony looks sad.

Her coat is rough and dirty. She looks

hungry.  runs up to the

 . The pony looks at Rusty.

4

Poppy tries to stroke the pony.

The pony looks frightened. "She's not very

friendly," says  . "Mr. Stone says

she's bad-tempered," says  .

5

Every day, Poppy goes to see the pony.

She takes  and carrots to the pony.

She always stays on the other side of the gate.

The pony eats from Poppy's .

One day, Poppy takes Sam with her.

But they cannot see the  anywhere.

The field looks empty except for a little

 .

Poppy and Sam open the gate.

Rusty runs into the field.  and

Sam are a little scared. "We must find

the  ," says Poppy.

8

Mr. Boot

I found the duck!

Poppy

I found the duck!

I found the duck!

Sam

Sam

apples

grass

stick

Poppy

I found the duck!

pony

Poppy

fence

I found the duck!

pony

I found the duck!

Rusty

I found the duck!

Mr. Boot

"There she is," says Sam.

The pony has caught her head collar on the

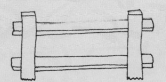 . She has been eating the

on the other side.

9

Poppy and Sam run home to Mr. Boot.

"Please come and help us, Dad," says .

"The pony's head collar is caught on the

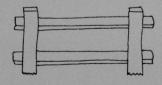. She will hurt herself."

10

Mr. Boot walks up to the pony.

Poppy and  watch him. He unhooks

the pony's head collar from the 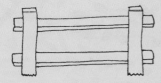 .

"She's not hurt," says Mr. Boot.

They start to walk home.

The  chases them. "Quick, run away!"

says  . "It's all right," says Poppy, patting

the pony. "She just wants to be friends."

12

Then they see an angry man.

It's Mr. Stone. "Leave my pony alone," says

 . "And get out of my field."

He waves his [knife] at Poppy.

Mr. Stone is very cross.

He waves his 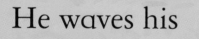 at the pony.

The  is afraid. "I'm going to get

rid of this nasty animal," says Mr. Stone.

14

Poppy grabs Mr. Stone's arm.

"You mustn't frighten the pony,"

she cries. "Come on, ," says

. "Let's go home."

The next day, there is a surprise for Poppy.

"We've bought the pony for you,"

says 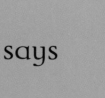 . "Thank you!" says Poppy.

Cover design and digital manipulation by Nelupa Hussain

This edition first published in 2005 by Usborne Publishing Ltd, Usborne House, 83-85 Saffron Hill, London EC1N 8RT, England. www.usborne.com